NUMBER FIVE ★ GHOST TOWN MYSTERY SERIES ★ CARSON CITY, NEVADA

# GHOSTOWNERS

# GHOST GIRL IN CAR Nº9

## BY CALAMITY JAN

don't, we shall run away." Tears welled up in her wide blue eyes as she held the only true friend she had left in the world close to her heart. "Now that Mama and Papa are in heaven, we have to stay together, Gypsy."

The scraggly dog held his beloved rawhide bone in his mouth and looked up at her with trusting eyes. *I'm with you. I hear every word. I understand.*

"The Orphan Asylum in Virginia City?" the conductor walked up and took the papers from her hand, furrowing his brows. "The Nevada Orphan Asylum?"

She nodded, straightening her wispy gold curls and tucking her leather suitcase beneath her seat. "Yes Sir," she replied with all the dignity she could muster.

The kind gray eyes widened with concern. "What will you do with the dog, child? Surely you know the Sisters of Charity can't allow pets in the asylum."

Jennica grew rigid, fighting the flood of fear engulfing her. "I will keep my dog, Sir. Perhaps you don't understand, but Gypsy and I shant be parted."

Gypsy laid his shaggy head against her thin woolen cloak and gazed up into her eyes brimming with tears, then dropped his beloved bone in her lap. *Don't be afraid, Jennica.*

*Believe.*

# Chapter One

"I can't believe this. It's *her*." Brooks steadied his tall frame against a brass rail, blinking in unbelief. "Oh my gosh, it's her!"

"Who? Whaat?" Meggie nearly fell over her mop bucket.

"The Ghost Girl! I—I just saw her in car N° 9—over there," he cried, pointing a trembling finger at the passenger car on display in the Nevada State Railroad Museum in Carson City. "I can't believe it." Brooks Jones started running toward the railroad car, his Nikes screeching on the polished floor.

Meggie's best friend Paige walked up from behind. "What's wrong with him?"

Twelve-year-old Meggie Bryson drew a deep breath and steadied herself against the mop handle. "He saw her. The girl."

"A girl? What's going on? Is he in love or something?" Paige Morefield's dark eyes flashed under the glare of the lights in the museum. "He's only sixteen. He's supposed to be working, not chasing girls anyway."

"Th–the Ghost Girl…" Meggie choked on her words. "He saw her in car N° 9."

Paige gripped her can of brass polish and watched Brooks unlatch the chain and step up into the passenger car on display. "Whoa! Are you talking about the legend of that girl they say is still riding the Virginia & Truckee Railroad? Like for over a hundred years?"

Meggie nodded and set down the mop, hurrying toward Brooks.

"This sounds like the next assignment for The Ghostowners," Paige said to Meggie.

"She's gone," Brooks told them the minute they entered the passenger car. "Poof. Gone. Just like that."

"Maybe you were just imagining it," Meggie said to him, glancing around. Car N° 9 had been built in 1873 and the museum kept it looking as good as its heyday years when it carried miners and workers to and from the mines and boardwalks between Reno, Carson and Virginia City.

"No. I saw her. Gold hair and wearing an old fashioned coat or jacket or something. I think she saw me, Meggie. She was so pretty."

"The ghost town detectives are facing a serious assignment," Paige said to Meggie, glancing around furtively. "You can get onboard with us if you want, Brooks," she added.

"Excuse me? What do you mean I can get onboard with you? I'm already onboard. I'm the only one who saw her." He hitched up his baggy jeans and frowned.

"Wait a minute," Paige stepped closer, holding her chin firmly. "If it wasn't for Meggie's aunt, we wouldn't even have this job volunteering at the museum and you, Brooks Jones, wouldn't even be hanging out with us."

"Or you."

"Okay, you two," Meggie put in. "We're all lucky my aunt is an archaeologist and needed to do some research here at the museum. That said, we can work together and figure this out."

"Starting with let's ask your aunt if she knows anything about the legend of the Ghost Girl and find the records that prove she existed," Brooks said, following them out of the passenger car and latching the chain behind him.

"I still think Brooks is too old to qualify as an authentic Ghostowner," Paige said to Meggie. "I think twelve or thirteen should be the maximum age."

"What are you going to do when you turn sixteen like me? Sixteen is not old," he said with a snort, catching up. "Don't forget my discovery at the Comstock Cemetery," he reminded her. "Remember the Haunted Horse of Gold Hill and the mystery you wouldn't have solved if it wasn't for me?"

Paige paused and turned to him, her short bob of chestnut hair flying like the mane of a young colt. "You have a point."

You got that right, he said to himself. His half-pint friend was beginning to get on his nerves, stomping around like a drill sergeant with boots way too big.

"We need Brooks," Meggie said to Paige, handing her the rag and polish. "He saw the girl. We have to start with that and work from there." She picked up her mop.

"Mr. Walker might also know quite a bit," Brooks said, shifting his focus away from Paige. "Since it looks like he's in charge around here, he might be the best authority on that legend."

Meggie nodded. "And Russ."

Paige agreed, thinking about the head volunteer at the museum. "Might be," she said thoughtfully. "Even though he is pretty old, I think he's addicted to trains which might make him our

9

best bet. Once he gets started, not even a locomotive can stop him."

Brooks bit his lower lip thoughtfully. "But maybe the Ghost Girl can."

# Chapter Two

Now officially a Ghostowner, Brooks Jones picked up his brass polishing cloth and worked his way along the rail toward the museum entrance where Russ sat at the Information desk.

"Hi, Russ."

"Well hello yourself, Brooks." The friendly volunteer with a full white beard smiled and looked up from a train magazine with his bright, energetic eyes. Dressed in the museum blue denim uniform, complete with engineers cap, Russ Tanner looked as though he had been around the place for a century or two. "Looks like you and your friends are keeping things nice and shiny around here."

"Yeah, we love trains. Thanks to Meggie's aunt we wouldn't have got on as volunteers if it wasn't for her." Brooks grinned, knowing they had a very cool setup. Aunt Abby was the perfect supervisor; just enough hippie with some archaeologist thrown in to create an ideal situation for ghost town detectives who preferred plenty of space along with important information. More times than not Aunt Abby got so involved in her research that she'd forget it was time to eat and go home. Meggie and Paige's folks back in Washington State would keel over if they knew how much freedom they had, but nobody wanted to rock the boxcar and ruin a good thing. It didn't matter to Brooks what his parents thought though, because he didn't have any. He was an orphan and pretty much on his own now. Getting on here at the railroad museum was the perfect way to end his summer.

"Got a question?" Russ asked.

"Oh yeah," he casually tossed back a tag of straw blonde hair falling over one eye, but his heart still pounded with the excitement of what he'd just seen in car N° 9. "Yeah, what do you know about that legend of the Ghost Girl?" Brooks asked.

Russ smiled. "Nobody knows much of anything except there have been accounts through the years that she appears in N° 9 now and then. That's about all I know. Why not ask Mr. Walker who runs the museum store?"

Brooks thanked him and then headed into the museum store next to the Director's office.

"What can I do for you?" Ms. Joslyn smiled from behind the counter.

"If Mr. Walker isn't too busy, I'd like to talk to him," Brooks said to the friendly lady who always seemed glad to help or answer any questions.

The retired school teacher picked up the phone and nodded. Her short crop of gray hair caught the sunlight as she ushered him into John Walker's office.

"Do you know anything about the Ghost Girl?" Brooks asked, casually hitching up his baggy jeans.

"Wish I did," Mr. Walker replied, scratching his dark hair peppered with gray. "Probably just a legend although some people swear they've seen her."

"I did," Brooks said to him, still trying to keep the excitement from exploding all over the office. "Ten minutes ago, but when I got into N° 9, she was gone." By this time, Meggie and Paige had caught up with Brooks and stood listening, their eyes wide and eager for more information.

"Is she trying to tell us something?" Meggie spoke first, bracing her tall, lanky frame against the desk.

"Maybe she is," John Walker said.

"Do we have permission to find out? You know—the typical things ghost town detectives have to do?" Paige asked, inching closer.

"I don't see why not," he replied. "It's been a mystery ever since I came here—ever since the museum was built. Passenger car N° 9 was for those who couldn't afford the more luxurious car; for the miners and workers traveling to and from the Comstock during the mining heyday in Virginia City. People only see her in that car, so we know she didn't travel first class."

"She was so pretty," Brooks put in. "Funny old clothes, though, so yeah, maybe she was kind of poor."

"Well," the store manager said, "don't let me keep you."

"What about our duties as volunteers?" Brooks asked.

"Secondary," he answered, getting up and ushering them out of his office. "Now go polish and mop or find the girl," he added with a smile as he tucked his keys into his blue jeans. "I'll inform Russ so you'll be free to do what you have to do."

Paige almost doubled over with joy the second they stepped outside the museum. "Does it get any better than this?" she laughed, throwing up her hands.

Meggie leaned against the outside door and shook her head,

her dark blonde hair catching the late summer wind dancing through the Carson Valley. "Probably not," she replied. "But we need more information if we plan to get anywhere."

"You mean Aunt Abby?" Paige asked, tucking her shirt into her ratty jeans. Although Paige Morefield was smaller than most kids her age, she made up for it with her confidence and strength.

"Yes," Meggie replied, "but only after she gets her nose out of her research. She made it clear she didn't want to be disturbed unless it was an emergency. And Paige, try to wear jeans that aren't so well air-conditioned. You've got more holes than I can count."

"These jeans are cool."

"Yeah, but we're volunteers in the Nevada State Railroad Museum and we shouldn't look like we just crawled out of a rat hole. Those jeans are cool if we're hiking or exploring or going to school, but not here."

Twelve-year-old Paige rolled her eyeballs toward heaven and sighed.

At closing, they gathered around Aunt Abby's Jeep and headed back to Virginia City, explaining what had happened and asking if she knew anything about the legend.

"No," Meggie's aunt replied, her wild wisps of gray-blonde hair flying in every direction. "I haven't heard but when we get back to the museum tomorrow, I'll look into it." She dropped Brooks off at the house where he'd been staying near Gold Hill, then drove to Jumbo Springs where they were camping.

And the next day she did just that. "I've spent a few hours researching the archives at the Nevada State Library and the records are spotty," Aunt Abby told them at lunchtime. "For over a hundred years there are only a few undocumented reports of a girl seen on the Virginia & Truckee railroad. Two reports say she appears in car N° 9 and then disappears. Not much to go on."

Brooks drew a deep breath and walked back into the museum. *But we'll find her. We'll find out why she keeps coming back. Maybe she's trying to tell us something. But why me? Why did I see her and not Meggie or Paige?* He paused, then walked toward the car on display, feeling honored in a way, wondering why she would appear to him and not Meggie or Paige? Or Russ. *Why me? I'm not important. Just a sixteen-year-old drifter. An orphan.*

*Why did I see her and why is something inside of me telling me I have to find her?*

# Chapter Three

Just before the Lakeview Station and tunnel, Jennica hankered for a bit of lunch. She reached into her pocket and took out a packet of carefully wrapped pasties and some tidbits for Gypsy that Mrs. Tankersley had prepared. Their neighbors in Reno had been kind after her mother died of consumption but 1873 was a time of terrible financial hardship for the country and friends apologized but explained that one more child to feed was impossible.

"The Nevada Orphan Asylum in Virginia City is our only hope, Jennica," her mother told her just before she died, her strength waning. "I have bought your ticket and all the papers are in order. The Sisters of Charity are expecting you." They held each other and cried a lot during their last days together and Gypsy scarcely left her bedside.

*I don't want to go there, Mama, but I won't say it because I can't bear to add to your sadness.*

Jennica gave the tidbits of food to Gypsy, remembering her mother's words as she watched her grow weaker and weaker with the disease in her lungs.

"The Comstock is rather wild with the clamor for gold and silver," she told Jennica, "but Bodie is far more wicked than Virginia City. At least you won't have to go there. Once you settle in at the orphanage, perhaps you can take flowers and visit Papa in the cemetery there," Mama added, trying to smile through her haze of tears. "Of course I'll be with him soon, so I suppose you can do as you please."

Jennica Teague listened to the V & T train blow its whistle, quickly brushing away a few unbidden tears. Thankfully, the miner sitting in the seat next to her hadn't noticed. Gently, she set Gypsy down at her feet and leaned forward to warm her hands by the stove in the center of the car. Jennica didn't want to live in Virginia City again but since she didn't have a choice, she knew she would definitely visit Papa's grave. Still, it was nearly impossible to understand why he had to leave her and Mama and die in the mines? *And now Mama.* Jennica swallowed a wretched knot of sadness, shifting her thoughts back to Gypsy and the important matters at hand.

She took another bite of Mrs. Tankersley's pastie, deftly taking out some mutton for Gypsy. Gypsy adored pasties, especially the meat and potatoes tucked inside the crispy pastry crust.

*Thank you.*

Jennica smiled down into the wide, expressive eyes of her little dog who licked his chops politely but with satisfaction. *You're welcome, Gypsy,* she said with the words inside of her that Gypsy understood, remembering how they all loved Mama's pasties. Especially Papa who came from Cornwall England where pasties were practically the most important food on any table or in any miner's lunchbox. The Cornish men were proud of their skills as hard rock miners and were in high demand in the Comstock where veins of silver and gold ran like rivers underground. Cornish men like her Papa were considered the best lode miners in the world.

Jennica remembered when Mama and Papa moved to Virginia City. She enjoyed almost everything except the loud noises of the stamp mills pounding out gold and silver ore day and night, but they were lucky to have a little house on B Street and enough money for food. She helped Mama wash and press the fine linens and silk dresses and waistcoats for the Mackays and other wealthy families while Papa worked in the Yellow Jacket Mine just down the grade at Gold Hill.

Every time she heard a whistle or a siren or fire bell, Jennica felt a shiver run straight to her boots, remembering that terrible day when a huge fire swept through the Yellow Jacket Mine and took her father away. She and Mama got the terrible news just after they had finished delivering some freshly pressed laundry to the Mackay mansion. After they buried him in the cemetery on the hill, they moved to Reno because Mama couldn't bear to live so close to the memories.

Gypsy jumped back into her lap with his beloved bone in his mouth, smiling about the pastie tidbits still decorating his whiskers. Jennica stroked him, remembering when they found him cold and shivering near a mine just above Virginia City. Even though it was a struggle to find enough food, they loved him and kept him anyway. Papa fashioned his splendid rawhide bone which he carried everywhere with deep pride. Papa was a skilled woodcarver as well as a miner and the day he gave Gypsy the bone was a day Jennica would never forget.

"Keep this bone always, Gypsy," Papa said, stroking him gently. "Inside I am leaving a blessing and a prayer for you and for

Jennica. Believe in miracles always. Keep this bone and the two of you will be safe."

*I will do this. Thank you.*

He was just a half-grown pup then, but Jennica heard him and knew he understood.

Suddenly the V & T locomotive's whistle brought her back to reality, signaling they were approaching the Lakeview stop. The whistle sent a frightful shiver clear down to the scuffed tips of her high-button boots, but she knew how to set the memories aside and do what must be done.

"This is the last stop before Carson City," Jennica said to Gypsy. "After Carson the train takes us on to Virginia City."

*May I get out for a few moments here?*

"Oh yes, of course I know you're hankering to take care of things," she went on, gazing out the window. "You won't freeze your paws here, though, Gypsy. Snow hasn't come yet."

"What, Missy?" the man beside her asked, leaning down and spitting into one of the fancy spittoons decorating the center aisle of the passenger car.

"Oh. Oh, I was just talking to my dog, Sir."

"Aye, Lass. I do that except I don't have a dog, so I just talk to meself."

She smiled, trying not to let her eyes fall on the wretched spittoon. Mama called it a cuspidor but Papa called it exactly what it was.

"Lakeview!" the conductor called out and then leaned over and spoke to Jennica. "We don't always stop here but today we have to drop off some supplies. Fifteen minutes to get off and stretch a bit."

Jennica hesitated before she took Gypsy outside, wondering if she ought to leave her suitcase unattended. It held her meager belongings which had scant worldly value, but her grandmother's Bible and the photographs of Mama and Papa tucked inside were more important than all the gold and silver in Virginia City.

"It's safe to leave it, Miss," the conductor said as though reading her mind. "It's my duty to keep things safe here. You and that little dog stay close now and be back when you hear my whistle."

Relieved, she stepped off the train and walked past the building to a splendid patch of grass and autumn leaves. "Stay close," she said with a smile, knowing he would. Gypsy never left her side.

Suddenly Gypsy turned, lifting his nose to the wind. Even with his little bone in his mouth, she heard the troubled growl.

"What's wrong, Gypsy?"

Without answering, her little dog took off running southward.

"No, Gypsy! NO!" she cried, running after him. Jennica watched the shaggy brown fur fade and blend with the windswept leaves and shrubs and tall grasses in the distance. "Gypsy! Gypsy! STOP!"

But her little dog paid no heed and before she realized it, he had disappeared. Terrified, she stopped, wiping a frantic sweat from her brow, fighting the confusion and fear strangling her. "Gypsy, where are you? What is wrong? Why are you running from me?"

Suddenly, she heard the conductor's whistle from behind.

"All aboard! Next stop, Carson City!"

"GYPSY!" she screamed, "Come back, Gypsy! The train must leave!"

"Missy!" the conductor called, hurrying toward her. "What has happened? You must come. The train is leaving."

"My dog ran southward toward the tunnel," she replied, her golden braid tossing wildly with the wind and turmoil of her desperate plight. "Please Sir, help me find my dog!"

"I'm so sorry," he replied, "but we cannot wait."

"Then I shall stay and wait for him," she countered. "Gypsy ran forthward for a reason!"

"Forgive me, child. Because of your age, I am required to see you to your destination."

"I am not a child!" she said boldly, her blue eyes flashing louder and brighter than the sky above. "I shall follow Gypsy and you will not catch me!"

"Dear Girl," he pleaded. "The Virginia & Truckee Railroad runs on a tight schedule. We cannot wait for Gypsy."

Suddenly, Jennica reeled around, grabbing her cloak with frantic hope as she listened to a faint barking in the distance. "That's him!" she cried. "Gypsy!"

The barking grew louder.

"Hurry little dog!" the conductor called, turning and motioning the girl to follow.

Gypsy barked wildly, racing toward Jennica, circling her even as she reached out to gather him in her arms.

"Come, Gypsy!" she cried, holding out her arms. "The train leaves now. We must hurry!"

Gypsy growled, and then backed up. *No. I cannot. Danger lies ahead. Danger, Jennica!*

"Danger? Oh, Gypsy! What are you trying to tell me?"

The conductor blew the whistle one last time. Jennica felt the knot in her throat begin to strangle her. "Please, Gypsy—come! Come to me!"

Her little dog ignored her plea and instead raced toward the tracks and began circling in front of the locomotive, barking frantically.

"No, Gypsy! Get off the tracks! GET OFF!"

The engineer noticed the dog and grabbed the cord, the warning whistle exploding like dynamite into the mid October day.

But Gypsy continued to bark and circle the tracks directly in front of the locomotive.

"Something is wrong!" Jennica cried, running toward the conductor. "Never has such a thing happened with my dog. Gypsy is telling us there is trouble!"

By this time most of the passengers had already boarded. The brakeman, who is the eyes and ears for the engineer, hurried ahead to thwart the dog who hindered the departure. "Outta the way, Buster!" the man cried, attempting to shoo the pup away. "Go now! Scat!"

"Something is wrong," she continued to plead.

The conductor adjusted his black cloth hat with patent leather visor and kneeled down to face the girl, listening.

"This has never happened before, Sir. Gypsy is telling us that something is very wrong ahead. He knew it almost immediately. He would never leave my side unless there is danger. I promise you this."

The conductor stood up and motioned for the brakeman.

Jennica followed them as they headed toward the locomotive, then rushed ahead to gather Gypsy in her arms, but the little dog would not. He didn't stop barking either, and now began to run ahead on the tracks, the small legs and shaggy body deftly leaping over each wooden crosstie.

She followed him on the tracks. "They won't run over us, Gypsy, but you dare not be sending all of us on a wild goose chase!"

Just around the bend she saw a tunnel in the distance. "The Lakeview Tunnel," she cried out. "I've only heard of it. Are you afraid of the tunnel, Gypsy? Is this why you're barking?"

Behind her she heard the voices of the conductor and brakeman and in front of her the little dog continued to bark and trot ahead. A frightening gradual darkness enveloped her once she entered the tunnel and then suddenly she knew. Smoke. The tunnel was on fire!

*Can you understand now, Jennica?*

"Oh Gypsy, yes! YES!" She reeled around and ran toward the light and the railroad men who were not far behind.

"A fire! In the tunnel!" she called out to them. "Can you see the smoke? If not, don't you smell it?" Gypsy circled her heels, staying with her now.

"Thank you so much, Gypsy." She gazed down and stroked

her little dog. "Oh thank you, Gypsy."

*You will be safe now, Jennica.*

After the fire had been extinguished, everyone called the little rag-tag dog a hero. A tunnel fire can be deadly for a train and the passengers. Gypsy enjoyed the great honor and kindness, especially the treats tossed his way that afternoon. Just as the conductor called "All Aboard!" and began to close the door on passenger car N° 9, Gypsy jumped out of Jennica's lap, running for the door and leaping off the train.

*My bone. I dropped my bone, Jennica. I must go back and get my bone.*

"No!" she cried, getting up. "Gypsy! GYPSY!"

But it was too late.

# Chapter Four

Brooks hung out around N° 9 every day after that, hoping the girl might reappear. Sometimes Meggie and Paige joined him, but mostly he stayed by himself, cleaning and polishing it until everything glistened, even the spittoons. About five days later as he oiled and polished the pot-bellied stove one more time, he sensed movement. He looked up and there she was, reaching toward the stove with both hands as though trying to warm her hands.

A great fear pulsed through him and made him shiver, although he was not cold. Stay cool, Brooks. Just act like nothing much is going on. Maybe she won't disappear this time.

*Please don't go.* He held her gaze and smiled slowly and she smiled back.

"It's kind of cold when I come here now," she said. "They don't stoke up this stove anymore. Maybe you can put down the polishing cloth and find some wood." She smiled shyly, tucking stray curls aside.

"Yes, I mean no," he replied, noticing she still wore that same thin coat and was shivering. "Here, take my jacket," he said, reaching over to his denim jacket lying on one seat and handing it to her. "I don't think they'll let us build a fire in the stove, though. We're inside a museum."

"A museum?" She took the jacket and placed it on her shoulders. "Pray tell, what is a museum?"

Brooks didn't know what to say. He didn't want to move or say the wrong thing, he didn't want to frighten her for fear she'd disappear again. "It's a place that takes care of things so they won't fade and be forgotten."

"Perhaps that's why I come here sometimes. Perhaps I feel safe here."

"You are safe here."

"I feel it."

"I saw you the other day and then you disappeared," he said carefully. "Why did you do that? I wanted to talk to you."

Her wide blue eyes filled as she gazed down, fidgeting with her small hands in her lap. She didn't reply.

"Why did you come back?"

"Because I need help."

He drew closer, wiping a nervous sweat off his jeans. "Maybe I can help you."

"Sometimes I am frightened here, though," she said to him, gazing around at the glare of the overhead lights and rafters of the museum. "Everything is different in this car now, but I am desperate. When I saw you the other day something told me that you would understand and help me."

"I will if I can," he said, his heart pounding.

"What is your name?"

"Brooks. Brooks Jones. Right now I'm staying with a family in Virginia City and volunteering here at the museum until school starts. After that I'm not sure where I'll be staying."

"I used to live in Virginia City too, but Papa was killed in one of the mines and then Mama died a few years after that. I don't have a family now."

"I don't either."

"Then you are an orphan, too?" She gazed into his face, into the trusting gray eyes beneath the straw-colored hair.

"Yes," he said.

"Perhaps that is why I felt the kinship then," she answered. "Perhaps that is why I am coming to you now."

He nodded, feeling her plea in the silence that stretched between them. "I want to help you."

She looked at him carefully, and then wrapped his jacket tighter around her shoulders. "My name is Jennica Teague and I have lost my dog, Gypsy." She quickly wiped away a stray tear with her hand and went on. "I am supposed to go to the Nevada Orphan Asylum in Virginia City but I will not go without Gypsy. I simply will not. I miss him terribly. Gypsy is all I have left and I must find him."

"I'll help you if I can, Jennica."

Suddenly Meggie and Paige came around the corner and called out to him. "Brooks? Time for lunch!"

"Later!" he called back. And when he turned around she was gone.

"Noooooo..." he groaned, slapping his hand against his forehead. "Jennica, come back! Come back!"

Paige stepped into the passenger car first. "Who the heck are you talking to?"

"The girl," Brooks said, picking up his denim jacket from the seat.

"Oh no," he's losing it, Meggie," Paige called down to her best friend. "He says he's been talking to her."

"The ghost girl?" Meggie climbed in and sat down, handing him his jacket. "*You talked to her?*"

"Yes and she was sitting in the very seat you're sitting in now," he said.

"Oh my gosh, this seat *is* warm." She jumped up and placed her hand on the cushion. "Are you kidding us, Brooks?"

"No," he said. "She came back and we talked."

Paige's chin fell. "Seriously?"

"Yes," Brooks said to them both, still overwhelmed at what had just happened. "Her name is Jennica. She's an orphan and she's lost her dog Gypsy. She's desperate and asked for my help." He wished his heart would stop pounding so loud.

"Well why didn't you help her?" Paige asked indignantly.

"Because you and Meggie came busting in and scared her off."

"Oh gee," Meggie said. "That's too sad."

"Maybe she'll come back," Paige put in. "If she realizes we're ghost town detectives she might not be so quick to leave. Did you tell her you're part of the team?"

"That is too stupid, Paige. She's from another time, another era. Her clothes are like old and weird with high-buttoned boots and stuff. The places she's lived in aren't even ghost towns yet."

"Whoa, she might be a ghost," Paige stepped back, her eyes as wide as two gold pans. "Our area of expertise is definitely ghost towns, not ghosts."

"She isn't a ghost, she's a girl. A beautiful young girl and she needs help." By now his pulse had begun to slow down.

"Do you think she'll come back and talk to you?" Meggie handed him a sack lunch.

"I don't know," he said. "Go back and hang out around the entrance. Try to keep any visitors as far away from this car as you can. Take them on tours of the other cars, the other engines. I'll wait and hope she returns."

Meggie's tall, angular frame backed out of N° 9, stepping down. "Let us know if we can help."

"Yeah," Paige agreed, following her back to the entrance where Russ sat at the desk. "We're a team and don't forget it, Brooks," she called.

Brooks frowned and then smiled at his friend. "Staying away is your job right now, Paige."

He sat back down in the old railroad car and waited.

And waited.

"Come back, Jennica. Please come back...."

# Chapter Five

Jennica stared out the window of the train as it gained power and moved toward the Lakeview tunnel, searching desperately for Gypsy. *Please God, help me find Gypsy!* she cried silently through her frantic tears. *And please stay off the tracks, Gypsy! Please!*

"I'm sorry. I'm so sorry we had to leave your dog behind," a voice behind her said. She turned and looked up into the kind eyes of the conductor.

"I must go back," she said to the man. "I will not go on to Virginia City until I find Gypsy. I have to find my dog."

He gazed into her pleading eyes.

"Please help me, Sir. Please—"

"What can I do?" He knelt down in front of her, perplexed.

Jennica gripped the metal arms of her seat and held herself steady. "Although I don't have the ticket, please allow me to return to the Lakeview station and get off. I'm sure my dog will have returned and is now waiting for me, Sir."

"But this is quite unorthodox, Miss. I might be fired for doing such a thing."

"He saved us, Sir. Gypsy saved us from entering a tunnel which was aflame. The train could have ignited and exploded if it wasn't for Gypsy's warning."

"I understand, but—"

"Don't we owe it to Gypsy to save him now, too?"

The middle-aged conductor shook his head and gazed around, but no one appeared to be listening. The man sitting next to her had moved to the end of the car where a poker game captured the men and one woman with a flouncy red satin dress and hat. The Conductor leaned closer. "Get out at Carson City and when no one is looking, walk back to freight car N° 1005. Pass a few lumber cars. You won't miss it. No livestock in it right now. Watch for the sacks of grain and bales of fresh clean hay and then climb in when no one's looking. Wrap yourself up in the hay with enough space to look out through the slats for Gypsy. You'll be well-hidden as we aren't scheduled to be picking up cattle or sheep for a few days. Stay on this train and we will travel on to Virginia City but eventually the train will return to Lakeview. Just keep out of sight when you get off. Hide your suitcase behind the tool shed at the Lakeview stop in one of the empty freight boxes tomorrow when you return, unless you wish to try keeping it with you. I will find you."

"Thank you, Sir. Thank you with my heart. I'm almost positive Gypsy will be there waiting." Hope filled her wide blue eyes.

"Be safe, Missy. You and your dog are deserving of better than all that has happened." He straightened his shoulders and walked into the small freight compartment and over to the conductor's desk, retrieving some papers and filling in forms as though nothing had happened.

She drew a deep breath of gratitude and turned back to search the landscape for Gypsy. In a few minutes she felt a tap on her shoulder.

"A wool blanket for your shoulders, Missy," he said quietly. "For the passenger's comfort."

"May I keep it over my shoulders when I get off in Carson City?" she asked, knowing it might get chilly in that freight car.

"Of course," he replied, lowering his voice, "and I'll see to it that we get you enough tickets so that you can get back in one of the finer passenger cars in a day or so without any questions. It will be more comfortable."

"Thank you so much for your kindness." Her face lit up with gratitude as she smiled. "But wouldn't a fancy coach be too grand for the likes of me? Aren't such elegant cars for first class passengers only?"

"You are first class, Missy." He smiled back into the face that appeared almost to be the face of an angel. A *beautiful child*, he mused silently, *and so undeserving of this sad fate.*

"In some ways you remind me of my Papa," she said, breaking into his uneven thoughts. "Before he died in the Yellow Jacket mine, he fashioned a fine rawhide bone for Gypsy and told him to keep it always and that if he would do this and believe, then we would be safe. Papa also tucked some miracles inside just in case we would need them. Gypsy understands everything, sir. He knew the bone was special but had to drop it in order to warn us—to save all of us from the fire. He only sets down his bone to eat or sleep or frolic and bark when we toss it."

"And you believe the reason he ran back the second time was to find the bone he'd dropped?"

"I'm sure of it," she said.

The conductor shook his head and thanked her for telling

him more of what had happened and for the honor of comparing him with her father.

She turned again, setting her sights on the landscape, looking for Gypsy.

He glanced down at his watch fob, then gazed out on the familiar terrain and realized they were nearing the tunnel. "Lakeview Tunnel coming up, then Carson City!" he called out.

Jennica turned and sat up straight, gripping her suitcase and preparing for what lie ahead. The locomotive's whistle told her it was now time to prepare and follow the kind conductor's instructions. For the first time the whistle didn't send frissons of fear down her back and into her boots. For the first time in a long time she felt hope.

The moment the train stopped at Carson City she quietly stepped off, gripping her suitcase in one hand and gathering the blanket on her shoulders in the other. Getting lost in the crowd long enough to slip away unnoticed should be quite simple, she thought, smiling at the woman in red satin who rushed past her with silk pantaloons flouncing like thistles in the wind.

"Excuse me," the woman said with bright red lips.

Jennica nodded and stepped off the train, reeling from the strong scent of perfume. Walking into the station, she filled her small copper jar with fresh water, then stepped through the crowd back out under the late afternoon sun and wind. *It's time,* she said to no one in particular, setting her small firm chin and gripping her blanket tighter around her shoulders. Jennica moved quietly through the crowd toward boxcar N° 1005, glancing back occasionally to make sure no one noticed. Her small boots moved sure-footedly toward her destination, passing a few cars hauling lumber for the timber lining in the mines or to feed the furnaces of the stamp mills in Virginia City and Gold Hill. Thankfully, the Washoe Zephyr wind swept down into the Carson valley at exactly the right time, sending leaves and twigs flying in all directions, creating enough disturbance to keep everyone focused on keeping their hats and bonnets on their heads or children near the skirts of mothers.

*Now,* Jennica said silently. With a deft swing of her arms, she tossed her bag through the open door of the car, stepped back and gazed at the imposing opening before her. The height of the doorway looked daunting; why even the floor of the freight car was almost as high as her head. She glanced both ways down the track to see if anyone was watching.

"Oh, God—give me angel wings!" she prayed. With a mighty leap, she pulled herself through the doorway and climbed into the boxcar. Heart pounding, she gazed around, her eyes adjusting to the shadows cloaking the sacks of grain, bales of hay and a few wooden boxes stacked with fresh produce and supplies. Deftly, she made her way through the bales and boxes to some hay tossed in a far corner, realizing she had found a splendid place to hide and wait. She opened her suitcase and retrieved the last of her food, settling back to eat the pastie.

"I'm so sorry I can't share all of this with you right now, Gypsy," she said, taking a few tidbits of mutton and setting them aside, "but just wait until I return to Lakeview. We shall have our party then!" She finished the pastie, wrapping up the leftover tidbits and gathering the woolen blanket around her, making herself as comfortable as possible.

The darkening night sky swallowed up the dusk as she burrowed in the hay with the blanket and before long, the clickety-clack of the wheels on the tracks beneath the boxcar lulled her to sleep.

At dawn, a sharp whistle awakened her. She shivered and blinked in the pale light, brushing strands of hay from her hair and clothing, then sat up and climbed up on a crate and peered out between some slats in the freight car. Jennica realized that her hiding place had served her well. Most of the boxes of supplies were gone, replaced by empty crates and barrels. No one had seen her. She had slept through the night in Virginia City and now felt the train picking up speed and heading down the grade towards Gold Hill and the Crown Point trestle. She drew back, not hankering to gaze down on the hoists of the Yellow Jacket mine near where Papa died, glad to leave this frightful place with over a hundred saloons, six police stations, four churches and the dreadful orphanage. "I don't hanker to come back here Gypsy—except to bring flowers to Papa's grave someday when I'm all grown up."

She shivered in the morning chill and wrapped the blanket tighter around her shoulders, focusing her thoughts back on returning to the Lakeview station and finding her dog. *I'm hurrying as fast as I can, Gypsy*, she said as the train snaked over the trestle and down the grade. *The conductor will help us. I don't even know his name but he is so kind and I know we can trust him.*

The bright autumn sun warmed her as the Virginia & Truckee train rolled proudly down the grade, the early morning rays reflecting off the shiny brass ornaments of a regal locomotive, its balloon stack sending clouds of exhaust across the sage and rock of the Comstock. Jennica waited patiently as it stopped at Mound House, drifted down the Carson River Canyon and then on into Carson City.

"Follow me, Missy," the conductor said, helping Jennica out of the freight car at Carson City. "We are moving to the baggage section of N° 9."

She nodded with gratitude and followed him, clinging to her small suitcase.

"I have found a large empty trunk. You will be safe and well hidden," he told her. "And much warmer. Quickly now so we will not be seen." He stepped up into the passenger car, reaching down and taking her hand and ushering her toward the baggage section with trunks and boxes stacked everywhere.

"Oh!" She paused and drew a deep breath. "I declare I think I already know about this trunk, Sir," she said to the man. "It's somewhat magical I think. Yet I'm not sure. Oh, such folly. Why am I having such fanciful thoughts?" She smiled furtively and climbed in.

He tipped his head curiously.

"I've been here before but I'm not sure when. Mayhaps it's because this trunk holds one of the miracles Papa tucked inside Gypsy's bone." She smiled up into his face lined with concern.

His heart lurched, watching her settle herself comfortably without so much as a breath of complaint.

"Thank you kindly," she added, pulling the top over her head.

"I will be just fine. You see, I'm in a very special place."

"This one doesn't latch so we'll just keep the top ajar," he told her, swallowing a huge lump lodged in his throat. "You'll have plenty of air. Next stop is Lakeview. I'll let you know when it's time to step off."

She nodded in the shadows and felt the train begin to climb upwards towards the tunnel and Lakeview.

Excitement filled her whole being until she thought she might burst as they finally rolled into Lakeview and came to a stop. She waited for the conductor, gripping her suitcase with small trembling hands.

"All clear," he said following her out of the car while workers loaded supplies and a few people milled around.

Heart pounding, she gazed around looking for Gypsy. *Oh my. Why didn't I think of it? Of course he's waiting behind the bunk house with that little bone in his mouth.*

*I can scarce wait to see you, Gypsy! I'm coming!* She wanted to cry out to the people and sky and glorious sunshine beating down on her golden braid and dancing autumn leaves. But of course she didn't. She simply held her excitement close to her pounding heart and waited for the train to leave.

The moment the Virginia & Truckee pulled away from the station, she hurried around to the back of the building. "Gypsy!" she cried out with joy. "I'm here!"

A dead silence and empty horizon gave answer.

*Where are you, Gypsy?*

Empty freight boxes lay like vacant, sun-bleached coffins against the back wall of the wooden structure. Her throbbing heart fell into her boots as she braced herself against the old building.

"No. No..." Jennica collapsed on the crates and dead leaves and cried. *Where are you, Gypsy?*

# Chapter Six

Jennica knew how to find Brooks. She crawled back into the trunk and returned to N° 9 a few days later.

"Oh—my gosh. Jennica. You came back." Brooks Jones almost fell over his big feet.

"Yes," she said quietly, sitting directly in front of the dastardly spittoon. "Please stop polishing this wretched thing and talk to me."

He dropped his polishing cloth and steadied himself, grinning. "I've been waiting for you."

"I'm glad because I need your help."

"Yes," he replied. "You need to find Gypsy."

"Yes," she said to him. "You didn't forget."

"No, I didn't. I couldn't. But, how, Jennica? How can I help you here in this museum where these old railroad cars and locomotives have been sitting around for some thirty years?"

"You can't help me here. You'll have to come back with me."

"Back?"

"Back in time."

"I wouldn't know how to do that." He swallowed his words carefully, his thoughts racing.

"Well, I do."

Brooks drew a deep breath. "Can we bring my friends?"

"You mean those two girls?"

"Then you've seen them, too?"

"I did, Brooks, and I don't mean to be rude but you and your friends wear such odd clothing and shoes." She stared at his Nikes with her wide blue eyes, and then looked up into his face. "The smaller girl with chestnut hair has so many holes in her pantaloons. I fear she must be getting wretchedly cold now that winter's coming. And your breeches are frightfully large. Do you fear they might fall off?"

"This is possible," he said dumbly, hoisting up his jeans with a quick jerk.

"Can I trust them like I think I can trust you?"

"Yes," he said. "Yes. We're like a team that solves mysteries. I think it works better when we're together. I think that if we're a team we have a better chance of finding Gypsy."

"All right," she said to him. "Get them, but hurry. We have nary a moment to lose."

Brooks leapt out of N° 9 and found Meggie and Paige in the museum store talking to some visitors. His frantic gestures and expression told them both to follow, which they did.

"She's back," he said breathlessly, "and she wants us to go with her and help her find her dog."

"Go where?" Paige skidded to a stop.

"I'm not sure. Back in time I think."

"Oh yeah. Back in time," Meggie almost fell over her sneakers. "Brooks, are you losing it?"

"No. No, I'm not. You can stay here if you want but I told her how we work best as a team and she agreed to let you come."

"I've always wanted to go back in time," Paige spit out the

words. "This is our chance, Meggie."

Meggie steadied herself and gazed into the passenger car.

"There she is!" Paige cried out, pointing. "I see her now. Oh my gosh, Brooks. She *is* real."

Brooks nodded, motioning for them to follow.

"Here they are," he said, unlatching the chain and climbing into the passenger car. Meggie and Paige followed close on his heels.

"I won't have time to mend her pantaloons," Jennica said, staring at Paige in her hole-studded jeans. "She will be frightfully cold in the valley."

"Oh, not a problem," Paige laughed, slapping her thigh as she climbed up the steps. "To us, jeans like this are totally cool."

"Cool? Yes. I'm sure they are cool," Jennica said to her, frowning in dismay. "Especially in winter of course. And the winter chill is coming."

"I'm Paige's friend, Meggie," Meggie Bryson said, reaching out to greet the girl wearing clothing older than the vintage rack at the Goodwill store.

Jennica turned and stared at the tall slim girl with dark gold hair and blue eyes. "Hello, Meggie."

Meggie smiled. "We're here because Brooks told us you want help finding your dog. We hope we can find him but first you'll need to explain a little more."

"You'll understand better when you get back to the Lakeview station," she told them, motioning for them to follow her into the baggage section piled high with old suitcases and trunks.

"Uh, you mean Lakeview where the trains used to stop

sometimes?" Paige asked.

"Yes," Jennica replied.

"I'm so sorry, but it's not there anymore," she explained. "That whole area got bulldozed when they built the new freeway over Lakeview Summit. There's a hiking trail where the V & T grade used to be, though."

"You'll see," Jennica told her, motioning for them to follow her.

Paige threw Meggie a wary glance as they followed her.

Jennica opened the leather-strapped lid of a large wooden trunk. "Follow me," she told them, climbing in.

"There won't be room for all of us," Meggie explained, drawing back.

Paige stood looking into the trunk and then reeled around. "She's gone, Brooks!" she cried, pointing at the ghostly haze of dust. "That girl disappeared…poof…just like that. Oh my gosh. My gosh!"

Brooks and Meggie peered over Paige's shoulder.

"Follow her!" Brooks said.

"You first," Paige stepped back.

Brooks Jones caught his breath and almost choked. "Okay. Yes. Why not?"

He crawled into the reddish-brown trunk edged in brass and leather and disappeared into the shadows.

"It's your turn, Meggie." Paige backed up slowly, staring dumbfounded into the ghostly haze.

"You're generally the brave one," Meggie said, gazing with glassy eyes into the old trunk.

"For most things but going back in time isn't one of them."

Meggie drew a slow, deep breath and then crawled in, Paige following her.

"Oh my gosh, whoa, oh my gosh!" Paige Morefield cried out, landing rear-first beside Meggie in a haystack on the back side of an old wooden tool house where Jennica and Brooks waited. She stood up and gazed around, wiping the dust from her jeans. "I'm so glad you're all here. Extremely glad. Whew." Wide brown eyes flashed like two round iron skillets.

"We're at the Lakeview train stop," Jennica said. "It's where I lost Gypsy."

"Oh," Meggie put in. "The Lakeview station? This is the old Lakeview train station?" She walked around to the front of the tool shed where some wooden crates were lined up. "This does not look like a train station at all."

"My gosh, Meggie. Don't you recognize the view?" Paige said, pointing. "There's Washoe Lake. That's why they named this place Lakeview. Of course things have changed since..." Paige sat down on one of the crates with a thud, scratching her head. "Wow, where did all the houses and the freeway go? I think I'm getting seriously confused."

Meggie frowned and sat down beside her.

"This is the train stop four miles north of Carson City," Jennica said to Paige. "I knew it would be easier for me to explain everything here instead of there."

"This place looks like it just stepped out of one of my history books," Paige said to her.

"1873," Jennica said to them. "The conductor told me this

43

wasn't a big fancy station like the one in Carson City or Reno. It serves as a maintenance station for the Virginia & Truckee trains connecting Reno with Carson City and Virginia City. They have a bunk house for the track workers, a tool house and the Track Foreman lives in that house over there," she said, pointing off to her side. "No one is here at the moment so we can talk."

"1873?" Brooks asked carefully, trying to keep his thoughts straight.

"Yes," Jennica replied. "The conductor showed me how to hide in the trunk in the baggage section of car N° 9 when I needed to get out of sight. He didn't know I'd already discovered the trunk and actually started using it when I needed to hide. The trunk has allowed me to ride that car anywhere, anytime. I didn't realize it would also take me to you at the museum. But I should have known," she said, smiling. "You see, it was another one of those miracles Papa tucked inside Gypsy's bone."

Brooks tipped his head, confused.

"Are we actually standing on 1873 dirt?" Paige asked, shaking her head.

The girl nodded.

"I am so impressed. So totally blown away."

Jennica gazed into Paige's wide brown eyes. "Blown away? There is no wind."

"It's something we say that means we're really freaked." Meggie put in.

"Freaked?"

Brooks frowned and cut into the conversation. "Tell us about

44

Gypsy," he said to Jennica. "Tell us where—and how you lost him."

Jennica sat down on a slatted wooden crate beside them and began to tell her story.

Paige shivered, gathering her knees in her arms. "I can hardly believe this," she said, listening to her unbelievable story, trying to keep the tears from exploding all over her face.

"You are shivering," she said to Paige. "I'm sorry your pantaloons are in such wretched condition. It is nearly November and the weather will be turning colder. Mayhaps you are feeling the chill even now."

"These are called jeans," Paige began to smile, running her hands down over the frayed hole-spotted denim fabric. "But I'm not shivering because I'm cold, Jennica, I'm shivering because this is such an unbelievable story."

"A most unusual blouse as well, Paige. I've never seen a blouse with a bird embroidered on the bodice. And such an odd bird at that."

"Oh, that's a Seahawk," Paige smiled down at her t-shirt. "Meggie and I are from Washington State and..."

"Washington Territory? Oh yes, a bird from the sea then? I've never seen such a bird. I declare, it seems quite wicked and beautiful both at once."

"Well, a Seahawk really isn't an authentic bird, Jennica. Actually it's the name of a football team in Washington Territory. . I mean, Washington State."

Jennica shook her head, confused. "A foot what?"

"GO SEAHAWKS!" Paige spit out the words because she

45

didn't know what else to do right then. "It's kind of hard to explain, Jennica. Actually, I don't think I can—in fact right now I think I'm totally confused."

"Which is why you need to be quiet, Paige, so that Jennica can finish telling us her story," Brooks said, the heat rising up his neck.

Jennica smiled and finished telling them all that had happened.

"And so the conductor and his wife sent food enough and finally let you stay with them instead of sleep in the hay or in the trunk?" Meggie asked.

"Yes, they have been so kind. His name is Mr. Lewis and he looks for Gypsy every moment he can. He and his wife Hattie have made it possible for me to ride back and forth between Carson City and Reno almost every day so I can search for Gypsy too. And now, come nightfall, Hattie picks me up in the carriage at Carson City and always has a warm supper and clean bed waiting." She smiled and brushed back a few stray curls falling from her braid glistening in the late morning sun. "Oh, so much more comfortable than with the hard boards and clickety clack all night long."

Brooks shook his head, unbelieving.

"And look at my fine new woolen cloak and leather shoes," she added. "Mr. Lewis and Hattie treat me almost as though I'm their own daughter. I'm sure Gypsy has found his bone because I'm beginning to feel more and more of those miracles Papa tucked inside."

Meggie glanced sideways at Paige, biting her lower lip and

wondering if the poor little dog could still be alive. Paige's wide glassy eyes told Meggie she was thinking the same thing.

"I believe in miracles," Brooks said to her. He didn't feel like explaining the details, but maybe someday he could tell Jennica about the miracle at the Comstock Cemetery in Gold Hill.

"So let's not tarry," Jennica said with a bright smile. "We must find Gypsy."

"Do you have a plan?" he asked.

"No, but I think the three of you are going to show me. Especially you, Brooks. You are an important part of the miracle. I'm sure of it."

Brooks swallowed hard. "Really?" he said, suddenly realizing the responsibility he faced. This was huge.

She looked up into his face and smiled again, waiting. Trusting.

"Yes, okay, but first we know Gypsy must be somewhere away from the tracks, somewhere maybe up one of the mountains to find shelter or food or maybe he trotted down to Carson City or on to Genoa or..."

The sound of horse's hooves growing louder and louder on the horizon made them all pause and look up. Brooks caught his breath. A stagecoach and driver coming toward them in a cloud of dust. For real. Not one of those stagecoaches you see in movies or a parade. *I can't believe this.*

"Whoa!" Paige almost fell backwards, grabbing the edges of the old crate for support.

"That's Hank Monk!" Jennica said. "He's heading directly toward this station, which is most perplexing."

"Who's Hank Monk?" Meggie asked.

"One of the wildest and most famous stagecoach drivers between Placerville and Genoa," she replied, staring at the four thundering horses slowing down now. "I recognize his stagecoach but I've never seen him this close before," she told them, her eyes lighting up. His silver-banded whip split the air like a shock of lightning. "I hear tell he detests the V & T Railroad because they're making it harder for him to make a living so that's why I can't believe he's stopping here."

"Need a lift?" the broad-shouldered man with a smartly-cropped beard called down from the carriage embroiled in dust. Silver Conchos circled the leather band around the crown of his Stetson hat and his sheepskin jacket almost—but not quite—hid his gun belt and holster. "Henry James Monk at your service."

"Yes—yes as—as a matter of fact, we do." Brooks tried not to choke on his words or trip on his big feet as he walked toward the imposing man in black denim trousers and black boots.

"Yes, sir—we do need your help."

## Chapter Seven

"Don't talk to strangers!" Paige choked out the words and backed away, nearly falling backwards over a spittoon.

Jennica turned to her and tipped her head curiously. "He's not a stranger in the Comstock," she said to Paige. "Mayhaps you don't know that Hank Monk is quite famous in these parts. Why his stagecoach even got Horace Greeley over the Sierra Nevada Mountains to a lecture in Placerville in record time."

"Alive," the rugged man smiled down from the coach, his feet firmly on the buckboard. "Now, let me repeat my question. Do you young people need my assistance?"

"Who's Gorace Heeley?" Paige held her ground.

"Horace Greeley," Meggie corrected, snickering.

"A real famous guy from New York," Brooks put in. "If my history is right I think he was a Politician and writer and I think he also ran for President of the United States or something like that."

"As famous as Abraham Lincoln and Pony Bob?" Paige asked, turning to Brooks.

"Possibly," Brooks said.

"Sir," Jennica walked up to the stagecoach and smiled at the driver, "we are most grateful for your offer of assistance."

"I seldom pay heed to anyone waiting at the V & T station

but four young people alone at a train stop with no Iron Horse due gives me concern," he said in a peculiar drawl.

"Thank you, Sir," she replied politely, "and we most certainly could use your help but I fear my pockets hold train tickets, not coins for your carriage."

"And no train is due until tomorrow," he said to her, getting out and walking around to open the door of one of the finest carriages in the territory. "I shant charge you a penny. Now give me your destination and I'll take you there."

"It's rather complicated, Sir. May I sit with you atop at the buckboard and explain?"

"Of course," he replied, motioning the other three inside the carriage.

Brooks' pulse raced with excitement as he stepped into the carriage. *I never in my life thought I'd be riding in an authentic 1873 stagecoach. Never. This is something none of the guys at school will ever believe. Not ever.*

Meggie followed and sat opposite him. Paige—whose eyes appeared wider than two oversized chestnuts—stepped in last, sitting down on the plush velvet seat beside Meggie.

"Watch for Gypsy every moment," Jennica called in before climbing up onto the front of the coach. "We must find him, we must!"

"Cut dirt!" Hank yelled, his silver-banded whip splitting the air. With a sudden jerk the restless horses began the journey, almost knocking the Ghostowners off their seats.

"Where are we going?" Paige choked on the words, gripping the gilded frame for support. "Yow. This is not exactly like riding the Greyhound bus on the Interstate."

"She's probably telling him about Gypsy right now," Meggie said, gripping the window frame and gazing out toward the timberline and the strange rock formations that separate the Carson and Washoe Valleys.

Brooks nodded, easing over to the opposite window and gazing on the dust-covered horizon. *This is beyond awesome.* "Yeah," he said, once he caught his breath. "Yeah, we're all here for that reason. I just hope this guy can help us."

"He might if he doesn't kill us all, first," Paige said, noticing they were moving away from the station, from the tracks.

By now they were bouncing around like puppets without strings. "Hang on," Brooks said. "I don't think Hank Monk is staying on the trail."

"If there even is a trail," Paige replied with a snort.

Meggie's tall, lanky frame bobbed in rhythm to the galloping hooves and sing-song of the huge wheels beneath them.

Jennica sat atop, holding on for dear life and telling him everything. Hank Monk's expression softened until he confessed finally that he had never been on such as an important mission as this. "We will search until dark," he told her, "and then I must take you and your friends to your destination."

Jennica Teague thanked him again and again, scouring the landscape. "Gypsy can't be far," she cried over the pounding of the horses' hooves. "We shall find him, Mr. Monk. We must!"

The afternoon sun fell too quickly behind the mountains as they searched the rocky terrain for the little dog. "Where now, Miss?" Hank asked just as the dusk settled over the valley and behind the Sierras.

"Mr. Lewis and Hattie's place near Carson City," she replied, her hopes falling. "North Carson just after the Lakeview tunnel. I will show you."

"Yes. I know Lewis. I know the place," he told her, cracking the whip into the air to move his team along. "He's a conductor and brakeman on the V & T. He and his wife are good people although I hear tell his wife Hattie is a dead aim with her frying pan if anyone crosses her." He smiled.

Jennica smiled back, then drew out a handkerchief, caught between sadness and gratitude for the kind man's assistance. "Where can he be Mr. Monk? I've searched for days, riding N° 9 back and forth, back and forth."

"Brisk up, Miss Teague," Hank said, "I will fetch you and your friends tomorrow. I don't have any assignations on my schedule. We will keep looking for your pup."

Jennica felt overcome with gratitude. "Oh thank you so much, Sir. Thank you kindly. I am feeling hope again." She gazed up into the brusque yet kind man's face with eyes that spoke to his soul.

"I will help you if I can."

Paige was the first one out of the stagecoach after Hank Monk pulled up in front of the simple wooden cottage at the edge of Carson City. "I think my aching bones and bruises will be permanent," she said to Meggie as she climbed out of the carriage behind Brooks. "Plus, where are we?"

"This is where I'm staying for now," Jennica told them as she climbed down. "The train conductor and his wife live here. And thank you so much, Mr. Monk," she called up, waving. "We shall see you in the morning at 8 a.m. sharp."

He nodded and smiled, cracking his whip as the stagecoach rolled off in a flurry of dust.

Brooks watched the awesome sight, hoping the excitement inside his bones would never go away. *So cool and maybe part of the miracle?* Brooks pondered the possibility.

"Let me go talk to Hattie about having you stay tonight," Jennica interrupted his thoughts. "I know it will be fine. She loves children and Mr. Lewis said that since I've been staying with them, she's been happier than she's been for a long time."

"Ooops, oh no. I'm sorry, but we can't do this." Paige stopped dead in her tracks, knotting her t-shirt nervously. "Jennica, I'm sorry, but we can't stay." She threw her hand against her forehead and gazed into the sky. "It suddenly dawns on me that we have to get back to the museum before they lock it up and Aunt Abby leaves."

"She won't miss you," Jennica assured her. "You can stay longer."

"Well, that just doesn't make any sense at all, Jennica," Paige said. "If we don't show up she *will* miss us."

"Paige is right," Meggie put in. "It's so cool to be here and ride that stagecoach but we have to get back, Jennica. If we're not there by the time the museum closes, my aunt might call 911."

"What?" Jennica loosened her braid and ran her hands through her soft cascade of curls.

"It's a number we call when we have an emergency," Meggie

53

explained.

"A number? Like calling out a number in a poker game? I don't understand."

Paige pulled her cell phone out of her pocket. "No, from our phone," she explained.

"What is *that*?" Jennica drew back, staring at the pink and white creature.

"It's a cell phone. A smart phone. We use these to talk to each other," Meggie told her. "I have one too," she said, pulling hers out of the rear pocket of her jeans. "We…"

"Hey, mine isn't working," Paige interrupted, punching in some numbers and holding it to her ear. "Dead as mud."

"There aren't any cell towers here," Brooks said, frowning.

"Oh yeah," Paige replied. "I almost forgot. We're standing on 1873 dirt. I thought maybe we could just call Aunt Abby and tell her we'd be late but I guess we can't do that since the phone hasn't even been invented yet."

Perplexed, Jennica shook her head and then turned and hurried into the cottage to ask permission for her friends to stay.

"I think all of this technology stuff scares her," Meggie said, staring at her smart phone.

"Could be, but what scares me is surviving without one," Paige said, putting it back in her pocket. "Another thing," she went on, pointing, "have you guys noticed that ancient Honey Bucket back there behind the house? I'm thinking like maybe we're looking at the possibility of no running water, no TV, no…"

"Yeah, Paige," Meggie said, "which is just one of the reasons why we have to talk to her about getting back. I hate to let her down, but Aunt Abby could have the Carson City Police Department out looking for us right now."

"I'm definitely beginning to get a little nervous about this going-back-in-time stuff, too," Paige added, limping up the steps. "We have to get back before the museum closes. Plus I think my bones are broken. Hank Monk is a crazy driver, isn't he?"

Before Brooks could reply, the door opened and a round woman with a gold braid wrapped like a crown around her head walked out. "Yah, of course your friends can stay, Jennica." She almost crashed into Paige.

"You must be Hattie," Meggie spoke first. "Sure is nice of you and your husband to help Jennica out. And to let us stay, except—"

"Plenty of room," the jovial woman went on with a smile that stretched from one side of her wrap-around braid to the other. "My good husband happens to be working on the late train to Reno tonight so there's plenty of featherbeds and vittles for all of you." She ushered them inside the small cottage brimming with tempting smells wafting from the wood stove.

"Thank you so much, M'am but we have to be getting back before the museum closes," Brooks said, turning to Jennica. He felt terrible. Guilty in fact. They hadn't done anything to help her.

Jennica turned and looked into his face her blue eyes wide with surprise. "Aren't you going to help me?"

"Yes, yes, definitely, but we have to get back before the museum closes. Meggie's aunt will wonder what happened," Brooks explained. "We need to explain everything to her and then we'll come back."

"I already told you that you will all be back before the train house—or that museum as you call it—closes," Jennica said to him.

"But, that's not possible," he replied.

"What Brooks means," Paige put in, "is that it's getting dark and we've been here longer than we thought and we definitely have to get back before Aunt Abby freaks out."

"When you crawled into the trunk in the baggage car, you left your time there," Jennica said to them.

Brooks stared at her. "Huh?"

"Seriously? You mean that when we get back, it's going to be the same time as it was when we left?" Meggie inched closer.

Jennica nodded.

"That doesn't make any sense," she said, shaking her head.

"Now I'm definitely going to freak out," Paige said, gulping so loud it sounded like a burp.

"Besides, you can't go back until we crawl back into that trunk on N° 9 and that train isn't due back in Carson for a few days," Jennica told them. "Mr. Lewis said it's in Reno getting some repair."

"*A few days?*" Meggie asked, nearly choking on her words.

"Yes," she brightened, "which gives us enough time to find Gypsy. Oh, I'm so happy you're here to help me," she said to her friends who stood with their mouths hanging open. "And Mr. Monk is helping us, too, Hattie," she added, turning to the

56

rotund woman leaning over the wood stove. A crackling fire in the huge stone fireplace warmed the simple cottage built of hand-hewn lumber.

"Eh, child?" The woman turned to Jennica.

"Hank Monk is returning with his stagecoach in the morning to take us back to the countryside to search for Gypsy. Isn't this splendid?"

"Hank Monk?" The woman nearly dropped the cast iron skillet. "Hank Monk you say?" She rushed toward Jennica, wiping her hands on her muslin apron. "Was that Hank Monk who dropped you off?"

Jennica nodded, her long curls almost dancing now.

"Bosh! Why Hank Monk thinks he's the biggest toad in the puddle, he does. Folks say he's the most daring of all the stage drivers in the country, the most reckless and dangerous and…"

"STRANGER DANGER! I knew it!" Paige exploded, interrupting the woman.

"Be quiet, Paige," Brooks said, nudging her with his elbow.

"…and anyone lucky enough to step out of his stagecoach alive is lucky indeed," Hattie finished, wiping her brow. "Now, enough of Hank Monk and that hog-wallow notion that's sure to create more problems than you've already got. Skedaddle and wash up and I'll rustle up some vittles in no time."

"I have to find Gypsy," Jennica said to Hattie.

The woman stared at the girl, her expression softening. "You poor child. I'm so sorry about losing that little dog of yours. Maybe he found a nice family in Carson," she said, "or romps in heaven with his little bone."

57

"No, Hattie. I feel the sunrise deep. I feel the hope. We will find him. We must all believe."

*Believe.*

The woman shook her head helplessly and turned back to the stove.

Paige drew a deep breath and gazed around the inside of the old house. An oil lantern sent eerie shadows across the wooden floor. *She is so brave.*

"Thanks, M'am," Brooks said, gathering his thoughts together. His stomach growled but even more important than food was the fact that Jennica was right. They had to believe. They couldn't give up hope.

They also needed to get some sleep if they planned on meeting Hank Monk at 8 a.m. sharp.

# Chapter Eight

*Riding in a Stage*

*Creeping through the valley, crawling o'er the hill,*
*Splashing through the branches, rumbling o'er the mill;*
*Putting nervous gentlemen in a towering rage.*
*What is so provoking as riding in a stage?*

*Spinsters fair and forty, maids in youthful charms,*
*Suddenly are cast into their neighbors' arms'*
*Children shoot like squirrels darting through a cage-*
*Isn't it delightful, riding in a stage?*

*Feet are interlacing, heads severely bumped,*
*Friend and foe together get their noses thumped;*
*Dresses act as carpets—listen to the sage;*
*"Life is but a journey taken in a stage."*

From *Six Horses* by Captain William Banning & George Hugh Banning. 1928

"Jennica," Brooks said as Hank's stagecoach pulled up in a flurry of dust the next morning, "may I please sit outside with you and Hank?"

Jennica paused, seeing this was important to her new friend. "There's scarcely room, but we can ask."

Hank Monk listened to her request, making room for Brooks

as Meggie and Paige climbed into the coach. "I understand this young man is quite important in your quest," he said. "He is part of the miracle, isn't he?"

"Yes," she said with great appreciation. "Yes he is, Mr. Monk."

Brooks swallowed a knot of undeserved thanks, hoping he could meet the challenge before him.

"Hang on," Meggie grinned, inching over to the window on the far side of the coach. "We're gonna make a little history here."

Paige curled her upper lip and rolled her eyeballs heavenward, gripping the frame securely so as to avoid a second layer of bumps and bruises.

"I'm going to circle around and take you on the stage route as much as I can so that the horses can rest and feed and get some water," Hank Monk told Brooks and Jennica. "This way we can hit two rattlers with one stone by alerting the stationmasters to watch for your pup. We'll also cover a radius surrounding both sides of the Lakeview tunnel so that you can get out and call for him. He might've found a warm cubby in the tunnel beneath that mountain. Nights are getting colder now and if someone hasn't already got him beside their parlor stove, he might be finding warmth and shelter in the tunnel."

Jennica listened closely and nodded, wrapping the sheepskin blanket he'd provided around her shoulders. *I'm coming, Gypsy.*

They scoured the dusty arid land, searching for the small brown dog and when they reached the north side of the Lakeview tunnel, Hank brought the rig to a halt. Jennica climbed out and hurried toward the black yawning mouth of the railroad tunnel.

"Gypsy!" she cried. "GYPSY!"

"Gypsy...Gypsy...Gypsy...." the hollow, mocking echo replied.

"Better not go any further, Jennica," Hank Monk warned, motioning her back. "Just keep calling. We'll wait."

Meggie and Paige got out of the stagecoach and gazed around. Paige rubbed her aching back and listened to her new friend calling for her dog, listened to the mocking echoes.

"It's kind of sad, isn't it?" she whispered to Meggie. "Do you think there's much chance he's alive now?"

Meggie shook her head, trying to keep the dark thoughts away.

"He's so little, Meggie," Paige went on. "Think about how many hungry cougars and..."

"Be quiet, Paige," Meggie said, walking toward the girl in the old fashioned dress and boots calling and calling in vain.

They finally left the north end of the tunnel and took the stage route around the mountain to the other side where Jennica called in once more. "Maybe he's closer to this end," she called back, her wide blue eyes filled with hope. "Maybe Gypsy didn't hear me from the other side."

"If he's in the tunnel, Jennica," Hank said, shaking his head.

"GYPSY!" she called over and over. "Are you in there? GYPSY!"

Brooks didn't get off the stage. He sat next to Hank with uneasy thoughts churning around inside. *I haven't done anything. She came to me first, believing I could help. And I haven't. I haven't done anything to help her find Gypsy. She's so scared.*

*It's bad enough being an orphan.*

"Yes," Jennica replied, stepping back finally and turning to Hank and the three ghost town detectives who stood helpless under the shadow of dusk. "Gypsy isn't in the tunnel." Her eyes filled with unbidden tears as she walked back to the stagecoach and reached for Brooks' hand, climbing on.

"Sorry, Lass," Hank said with more sincerity than he was accustomed. He took the rig at a slow pace back to the Lewis cottage, wishing he'd been able to help.

Paige didn't care if she limped and ached for a week and told Meggie she'd never complain about stupid, selfish things again. "We don't even know how lucky we are, Meggie."

Meggie nodded in agreement, knotting her long dark-blonde hair in a ponytail. "I feel so bad for her."

"I don't even care if I have to use that disgusting chamber pot anymore," Paige went on. "Or that wooden honey bucket in their back yard that smells worse than a thousand cow pies."

Meggie agreed. "We're pathetic, Paige."

"I have to get back on the line early tomorrow," Hank said to Jennica as they drove up to the cottage in Carson City. "I'm so plagued sorry we couldn't find your pup but I promise that I'll alert the stationmasters from here to California. We'll all be watching out for Gypsy."

Jennica nodded and climbed down behind Brooks. "Thank you so much, Mr. Monk," she said, reaching for her hankie in the pocket of her cloak. "I cannot tell you how most grateful I am that you tried to help me. We shant despair. We shall find Gypsy."

"You are a fine young lady," Hank said, watching the girl struggle to keep the tears from falling all over her cheeks. "Gritty and courageous. I'm proud to have the honor of meeting you."

She smiled through her tears and waved. "Thank you, sir."

Brooks unlatched the stage door for Meggie and Paige, wishing everything had turned out differently.

"If I hear anything," I know where to come," Hank Monk said, taking off his hat and shaking his head. "In the meantime, if you need me, send word and I will come."

The instant they walked into the house Brooks knew something was terribly wrong.

"Mercy! Mercy!" Hattie burst out, wringing her hands and knotting her muslin apron in despair. "It is dreadful. Dreadful..."

Jennica ran up to the woman. "Pray tell, whatever has happened?"

"They have come for you, Jennica."

A silence as deadly as a stealthy rattlesnake hit the room.

"Wh–who has come?" Brooks spoke first, breaking the stranglehold of fear gripping them all.

"Representatives from the Children's Asylum in Virginia City," she said, reaching for Jennica. "Oh child—"

"No! NO!" Jennica cried out.

# Chapter Nine

"I shant go to the Orphan Asylum!" Jennica cried, angry tears stinging her eyes. "I shant, Hattie!"

"They are returning tomorrow to fetch you," the distraught woman told her. "I begged them to let us keep you but they refused."

Brooks backed up, fear and anger surging like a Zephyr wind inside of him. *Tomorrow. No...*

"They had been searching the trains until someone told them you were staying with us," she went on despairingly. "They thought I might be hiding you. I told them you were out searching for your lost dog."

"What did they say?" Meggie asked.

"They said it's just as well the dog is gone because you wouldn't be allowed to keep him at the orphanage." She blew her nose, still pacing.

"That settles things, then, doesn't it?" Jennica cried, her small fists knotted with anger. Fear. "I shall never live in that wretched Children's Asylum! Never." She reeled around and faced Brooks, her eyes flashing.

"Let's get Hank to take you somewhere. Anywhere," he said to her. "You have to hide."

"Hank?" Meggie put in. "But, how do we find him? He didn't tell us where he was going."

"You can't just run, Jennica." Hattie hurried toward her. "We must find a way. We have the night to ponder this and perhaps by morning we shall find our answer." She gathered Jennica in her arms, feeling the terrible sobs against her muslin dress, against her heart.

Later that night, Brooks crept down from the attic after Hattie extinguished the last oil lantern and closed her bedroom door behind her. He slipped on his jacket and hurried out into the darkness, thankful for the scant light cast by the moon. Zipping up his jacket, he ran toward the flickering lights of downtown Carson City in the distance.

Before long he reached the Stiffhorn Saloon on the north edge of town. A rustic sign hung askew over the rough-hewn boardwalk and a few horses tied to the hitching posts nickered under the moon. Breathless, sweating, he burst through the door. "Hello!" he called to the bartender serving a mug to a leather-clad man draped over the bar.

"You're too young to be here, Boy," the bartender said with a snort. "Go home where you belong."

"There's trouble Mister," Brooks replied, breathless. "I need your help."

"Aye? Who can help? Look at these poor whittled souls lying around this rumhole. Nary a one good enough for more than stumbling back to their flea traps by dawn at best."

"Please, Sir. A girl is in terrible trouble," Brooks pleaded.

A voice spoke from a smoke-filled corner of the room behind him. "Trouble you say?" The man got up and walked toward Brooks, his leather boots with steel-trimmed heels thumping across the rough-hewn floor.

"Aye Bob," the bartender chortled. "When did you mosey in?"

"Haven't been here long," he said.

Brooks focused his eyes on the man walking toward him who looked like the most authentic cowboy he had ever seen in his life. He trembled with hope.

"Robert Haslam, here," he said to Brooks, reaching out a leathery hand.

"Brooks Jones, sir."

"I hear you've got some trouble?"

"Yes. I need for someone to find Hank Monk."

"Hank Monk, you say?" The man tipped his head curiously, slipping off his leather hat and scratching his head. "Monk isn't an easy dude to track down, young man. What's the emergency?"

Brooks explained as much as possible, his sweaty hands and brow betraying his growing tension. "Hank Monk is our friend and he will help us," he finished. "We have to find him."

"If I do find him, where will he meet you?" the man asked.

"Here. Here at the Stillhorn."

"Here?" the dark eyes grew wide with skepticism.

"Yes," Brooks replied. "Can you help us, Mr. Haslam?"

The man shook his head and then nodded. "Reckon I can try," he told Brooks.

"I will bring the girl here then, and thank you, Sir. Thank you so much."

Brooks followed the man out of the saloon and watched him

deftly untie and mount the finest steed he'd ever seen.

"Bring her back here then," Haslam called above the restless hooves. "I'll do what I can."

"Thank you," Brooks called back, turning and racing back to the small house on the outskirts of town.

"Meggie...Paige...Jennica..." he tiptoed into the cottage and crept up the stairs, opening their bedroom door. "Wake up," he whispered, closing the door quietly behind him.

Jennica stirred beneath the featherbed, a pale light trickling through the lace curtains. "Yes? What is it?" She brushed her curls aside and wiped the sleep from her eyes.

Paige snorted and snored on, scrunching herself deeper beneath the blankets of the old brass bed the three girls shared.

"We're going to leave. Tonight," Brooks said to them. "Get your things. I'll try to find some paper and leave Hattie a note."

"Whaaa?" Meggie sat upright, blue eyes flashing in the moonlight, her hair askew.

"Shhh!" Brooks gestured, still whispering. "Wake up Paige and be quick. I've found someone who is going to get Hank Monk to meet us. Bring warm jackets or blankets and pack your suitcase, Jennica."

After Brooks finished the note to Hattie explaining the situation, he followed the girls out on to the porch. "We're heading back to Carson on foot where I'm hoping Hank will meet us. Let's go," he said, reaching for Jennica's suitcase.

"But, how did you find him?" Jennica asked, hurrying down the steps.

"I didn't," Brooks told her, "but I found someone who might.

This cowboy guy has gone to find him and bring him to the Stillhorn where we'll meet."

"The *Stillhorn*?" Jennica stopped short.

"Is that an all-night diner or something like that?" Paige put in, wrapping a light blanket tighter around her shoulders.

"No," Jennica replied. "No, but I hear tell it's a rather notorious saloon. A bit rowdy and wicked, isn't it Brooks?"

"It was the only thing open," Brooks said. "And it was almost empty when I got there. We're lucky I found anything. Maybe there were a few more places open, but I hit pay dirt when I met that cowboy guy. Almost like a miracle, actually."

*A miracle.* Jennica nodded and hiked on, her hopes rising.

"So who is he? Who's the rider that's gone to get Hank?" Meggie asked, staying close on his heels.

"A Mr. Haslam," Brooks said, leading the way toward the flickering lights of Carson. "A Wyatt Earp–John Wayne type of guy. You should have seen his horse and the way he cut dirt and took off. If anybody can find Hank, I'm thinking this guy can."

Before long they reached the Stillhorn Saloon.

"What's this?" the bartender called out from behind the bar. "What are you doing back here young man? And what in tarnation gives you the nerve to bring more young whippersnappers to my place of business? It's past midnight. This is no place for the likes of you all."

"Sir," Brooks said, "Mr. Haslam is bringing Hank Monk here to meet us."

"Hank Monk?"

"Yes, he's our friend. He will help us."

The man looked at Jennica whose golden hair and angel-face seemed badly out of place in his establishment. "Is that the girl who has the trouble?" he asked Brooks. "The one you said who needs the help?"

Brooks nodded.

"I see," the man said, running his hands through his thinning hair. "Well, if anybody can find Hank Monk, Robert Haslam can."

"Robert Haslam?" Paige stepped toward he bartender. "The famous Robert Haslem? Are you talking about the guy they call Pony Bob?"

The bartender nodded.

"Whoa," Paige turned to Brooks. "You found the best."

Brooks' chin dropped. "Huh?"

"This is too cool. Pony Bob is probably the most famous Pony Express rider of all time," she said.

"How do you know that, Paige?" Jennica asked.

"He's in all of our history books," she told her. "His greatest ride was 120 miles in 8 hours and 20 minutes while wounded, carrying Abraham Lincoln's Inaugural Address. Another trip set the record; 380 miles round trip. This guy is seriously famous."

"Your history books tell of this man?" Jennica asked. "Why the Pony Express rode close to the time when I was born in 1860."

"I did a book report on Robert Haslam," Paige said. "Buffalo Bill paid for Pony Bob's headstone. He died a poor man."

"Robert Haslam dead? Aye, you're mistaken young lady," the bartender cut in. "Pony Bob is not in some Bone Orchard smelling daisies upside down. As a matter of fact, I'm hearin' a familiar tangle of hooves which tells me he's returning and very much alive."

Jennica ran outside, her heart pounding.

# Chapter Ten

"He's on his way!" Haslem called out, dismounting his horse. "Monk will be here shortly."

"Oh my," Jennica cried out, "Thank you, Sir. Thank you for helping me."

Robert Haslam paused and looked down at the girl with the soft golden curls beneath the gaslight lantern. His expression softened. "Are you an angel?"

"Actually," Paige said, "she's a ghos..."

Meggie nudged Paige with her elbow. "Yes," Meggie cut in. "She is an angel, Mr. Haslam."

Brooks nodded in agreement. *He's right. He and Meggie got it right.*

The rider shook his head, then gathered his wits. "McGee?" he called, barreling through the doors. "Prepare some cider and vittles for these young folk. They have a journey ahead." Haslam threw some coins on the counter. "Be quick. Monk will be here shortly."

By the time they finished the cider and sausage, Hank Monk pulled up in a cloud of dust. *Here we go*, Brooks said, setting down the mug and getting up. He listened to the familiar crack of the whip split the air, signaling the team to a halt. Relief flooded his senses.

"Thank you so much," Jennica said first, hurrying across the room and reaching for the rough hand of Pony Bob. "And you, Sir," she said to the bartender, "your kindness shan't be forgotten." Her smile practically lit up the saloon. Everyone wished her well and swore themselves to secrecy.

Brooks, Paige and Meggie added their thanks and hurried out to meet Hank Monk under the slice of moon.

Hank jumped off and opened the door of the stagecoach, urging Meggie and Paige inside. "Jennica and Brooks will sit atop with me and give me the details," he said to the girls, grabbing some wool blankets for their shoulders.

"The people from the Orphan Asylum have come for me," Jennica told Hank. Her eyes brimmed with unshed tears and fear of the unknown.

"They're coming for her tomorrow," Brooks added, feeling some of those same fears and uneasy memories welling up inside of him as well. "We had to leave."

Hank took the team and began a journey south toward Genoa. "What of the poor, kind woman who will be frantic upon awakening to an empty house?" he asked, arching a dark brow beneath his Stetson. "Am I to be found guilty of kidnapping helpless children?"

"Hattie?" Brooks put in. "I left her a note and told her we would be safe and bring Jennica back. I told her to tell them she had run away because she couldn't keep her dog. Which is true."

Hank nodded. "All right then," he said sending his whip into the air like a shock of lightning. "We're heading for Diamond Valley."

"Diamond Valley ? Where is that, Sir?" Jennica asked, hunkering down against the wind and cold thrusting itself upon them like a sudden storm.

"Five miles southwest of Genoa."

"Genoa?" Jennica asked.

"I'm surprised at you, Child," Monk snorted, "don't you know that Genoa was the first town established in all these here parts? Why, it's the oldest town in Nevada. Now hold on," he said. "You will find out soon enough."

## Chapter Eleven

After a long ride, Hank's rig pulled up in front of a finely built ranch dwelling at the foot of the Sierra Nevada mountains.

"Well if it isn't Hank Monk," a robust woman came out onto the porch to greet them, holding the hand of their young son. "What gives us the pleasure?" Her tall, slender husband followed, slipping on his Mackinaw jacket and wide-rimmed hat. Nordic blue eyes crinkled above the welcoming smile of the man with a carefully trimmed beard and gray-flecked hair.

Hank Monk stepped down and introduced the four young passengers to the woman and her husband and son, Arthur. Distracted, the six-year-old boy scurried down the steps with his dog, running into the fields of grain and livestock surrounding the ranch. "Agnes—Snowshoe, meet my new friends."

"Snowshoe?" Paige interjected, trying to keep her balance from the wild ride and her aching bones.

"Snowshoe Thompson," Hank replied with a chuckle. "Actually John to most of us. Carried the mail and much-needed supplies between Placerville California over the 7,500 foot passes of the Sierra Nevada mountains to Genoa on his homemade snow-shoes for twenty years. Never paid one cent for his mail services, mind you. Likely he won't tell you he's become a legend in these parts."

"Stop the nonsense and tell us why you've come," the kindly

broad-shouldered Norwegian said, reaching out and shaking the hand of his friend Hank.

"Jennica Teague has lost her little dog Gypsy and we need help finding it," Hank told him. "We know you travel all over these parts and your help is much needed John."

"Gypsy saved the train near the Lakeview stop," Jennica stepped forward, drawing her cloak tighter against her small frame. "There was a fire in the tunnel and he warned everyone. But now he's disappeared and I must find him."

"Fire, eh? Ya, it happens in the tunnels now and then," the man said, kneeling down and questioning the girl further, his clear blue eyes gazing into hers with kindness. "Then it was your little dog that gave warning in the tunnel at Lakeview? Your doggie saved the train?"

Jennica nodded, explaining her plight and telling them everything she knew. Her wide eyes filled as she tried to keep her heart from exploding. "Gypsy is practically all I have left."

"They won't let her keep her dog in the orphanage in Virginia City," Brooks put in, "so things are bad all the way around."

"He's little and brown and shaggy," Paige added.

Meggie nodded. "Plus he'll be carrying a bone. "The bone is important Mr. Snowshoe."

The kind-hearted man stood up finally, shaking his head.

Brooks noticed how carefully he listened to Jennica's story, yet he wondered how this man could help.

"All I ever carried through the wilderness besides the mail was some dried sausage or jerked beef, some crackers, matches and my Bible," Snowshoe said. "Grizzly bears, mountain lions and wolves roamed my path and when a storm hit and kept me back, I'd find a flat rock, clear it of snow and dance until it passed."

Jennica gazed into the man's wind and sun-weathered face and listened carefully.

"I think, Miss Jennica, that you are in a great storm now."

She nodded into the face and eyes of the wisdom, her heart groping for understanding. "Find a flat rock and clear it of snow and—dance? I don't understand, Sir."

"No matter how hopeless and terrible the storm, we shall do everything we can to clear the rock and prepare for the dance."

Hank Monk pulled out a handkerchief and wiped his eyes in an uncommon burst of emotion. "We have work to do," he said to his friend.

"Ya. Ya," the kind man said to Jennica. "All of us are going to do everything we can to make a way to find your little dog Gypsy."

Hank nodded, turning away and blowing his nose.

"You are so kind, but I don't feel like dancing, Sir."

"Neither did I," Snowshoe said, gazing into the face of innocence. "But the dance is the most important thing."

She brushed a few stray curls from her wide, questioning eyes.

"Excuse me for busting in, but dancing doesn't really make any sense right now, Mr. Horseshoe," Paige said to the man.

"Snowshoe," Meggie corrected, frowning and nudging Paige with her elbow.

"Working hard to find Gypsy makes all the sense in the

world, though," Paige added. "And we definitely could use more help, that's for sure."

*What does he mean?* Brooks wondered. *What is he trying to tell us?*

"Why should one dance in the storm, Sir?" Jennica went on, struggling to hold back unbidden tears. "Storms are dismal. I don't find joy in such things, Mr. Thompson, and certainly do not wish to dance."

"Because when all seems hopeless, then is the time to believe—the time when miracles might happen."

"Believe?" Jennica felt the strength of his words rushing over her like a sudden Zephyr wind. She turned and walked away, letting the tears come now—letting the hurt and fear explode into the Nevada sky and earth around her.

*Oh, Papa. You told Gypsy and me the same, didn't you? You tucked miracles into Gypsy's bone and told us to believe, didn't you? Papa. Mama. Gypsy. This is more difficult than anything I have ever known but I shall Believe.*

*I shall dance.*

When her heart quieted under the afternoon sun, she returned to the ranch house where Hank Monk and Snowshoe Thompson sat with maps and notes and plans.

"We are going to do everything we can to find Gypsy," John Thompson said to her, looking up from the maps. His kind smile told her she could trust him.

His smile filled the room and Jennica knew the dance had

already begun. She smiled back at the two men who would leave a heartfelt mark upon her life, two new friends who would go on to make history.

*But what is going to happen to Jennica?* Brooks wondered, struggling with the harsh reality. Even though he didn't like to dance, watching these men make plans to find Gypsy made him want to try. Still, some facts couldn't be swept off—or under the rock. "If we take Jennica back to Carson City, the men will come and take her away to the orphanage," he said to Hank Monk and Snowshoe Thompson. "And even if you do find Gypsy, she won't be able to keep him."

"I've already decided she is to stay with us until her safety is secured," Agnes told everyone. "Hank will take the three of you back to the Lewis home in Carson City," she said, turning to Brooks, Meggie and Paige. "He will give the Lewis' the quiet information that Jennica is in safe care for as long as is necessary."

"Oh—" Jennica threw her hands over her mouth with joy. "Oh, thank you. Thank you so much."

Brooks shook his head. "I need to get this straight. Back to the Lewis' and then what?"

"You, Meggie and Paige must board the Virginia & Truckee passenger train tomorrow at the Lakeview station," Jennica said to Brooks. "Get on car N° 9 and go back to the baggage section. You know what to do. Find the trunk that will take you back to the museum."

"Yes," Brooks said with a big gulp. "Yes, Jennica."

"I shall let you know when I find Gypsy." Her smile melted him and everyone standing there.

*But I don't want to go back.* Brooks turned away and struggled to keep his feelings inside. *I don't want to leave you here, Jennica.*

Hank Monk checked his pocket watch. "We must leave. I have assignations," he said, hurrying them into the stagecoach. "I will get you back to the Lewis place and return in the morning to fetch you so that you will not miss the train."

The three ghost town detectives hurried into the stagecoach, saying goodbye to their friends, but especially to Jennica.

"We will wait for word about Gypsy," Meggie said to her. "And we will dance, Jennica."

"Yes," Paige added, "and I am definitely going to work on my dastardly outrageous pantaloons. No holes next time." She smiled, trying hard to keep her tears from exploding all over her face.

Jennica waved and threw them kisses. "You shall see me again. And Gypsy!" Her huge blue eyes filled as she turned to Brooks.

*Will we, Jennica?* Brooks couldn't say the words out loud for fear it would never be so. His heart felt heavier than he had ever known. He felt as though he was betraying her. Letting her down. "Will you–tell us?" he asked finally, groping for the words.

"Yes," she said to him, trying to smile through eyes glistening under the sun. "Wait for us in the museum. Car N° 9."

"Us?" It was Paige now.

"Gypsy and me."

"But we have to leave the museum soon," he said, his words

knotting up deep inside. "Can you let us know in time—before we go home?"

Jennica nodded and waved, the breeze sending her golden hair flying in every direction. "Yes," she said.

*Home?* Brooks turned away and got into the carriage. *Where is home?*

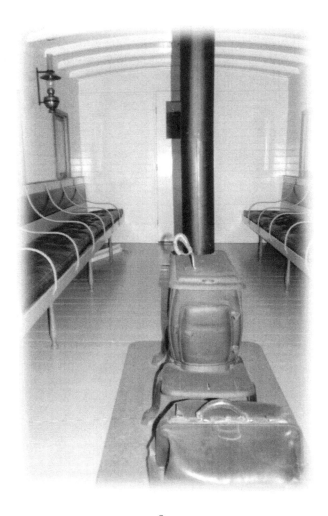

# Chapter Twelve

Brooks tried to stay busy in the museum, but it was hard to keep his mind off Jennica, wondering if she was okay and if they found Gypsy. None of them had seen her and in a few more days he was going to have to leave and go back to school and his life in Virginia City. Meggie and Paige had to return home to Trout Lake in Washington State with Meggie's Aunt Abby.

"I keep hanging out around N° 9 but she's not there," Meggie said to them late one afternoon just before closing.

"She promised she'd tell us when she found Gypsy," Paige added, trying not to let the sadness creep into her words. "And we told her we'd keep dancing." Paige Morefield leaned against N° 9. "It's hard when you feel scared."

Meggie agreed. "Yeah. Who feels like dancing?"

"I guess she just hasn't found him yet," Brooks said to them. He didn't say any more because he felt scared, too. Maybe it wasn't going to happen. Maybe Jennica lost her little dog forever and maybe she would have to be returned to the Children's Asylum. He felt sick inside.

"But that was like over a hundred years ago, Brooks," Paige replied.

"And what's going to happen to her?" Meggie said. "Will Hattie and Mr. Lewis get to keep her or will the authorities force her to go to the orphanage? Do you think those people from the orphanage came right after Hank took us to the train?"

"Maybe she'll stay hidden at Snowshoe's ranch until everything dies down," Paige said. "I think they'd keep her, don't you?"

Brooks didn't have an answer. He just hoped for the best but who knew? She told him to wait at the museum and they were doing that but they had to leave soon. The weight of sadness felt heavier and heavier on his shoulders. He tried not to let Meggie and Paige know how hard it was to be an orphan; to lose your parents and then lose even more. He choked back his fear as he thought about her losing that little dog along with everything else. Gypsy was all she had left.

Meggie and Paige shrugged sadly and walked away. Brooks glanced back at car N° 9 one last time and then followed them toward the door. It was almost closing time.

"I'm going back," he said to them both, his gray eyes flashing.

"What?" Meggie turned, nearly falling backwards.

"I'm going back to help her. I'm going to stay."

"Seriously?" Paige sputtered. "You mean stay in this museum?"

"No. I'm going back. Back in time."

"Oh my gosh," Meggie cried. "But why, Brooks?"

"I want to help Jennica and maybe find my family," he said, backing up. "There's no reason for me to stay here."

"Wait a minute, how can you find your family? They're all dead. You're an orphan, Brooks," Paige said to him.

"They're not all gone if I go back in time," he told them.

"This is way too freaky," she replied, knotting her shirt with sweaty hands. "Seriously, this doesn't make any sense at all."

"Maybe I can change history. Maybe I can find John and Henry Jones and warn them not to go out in that blizzard. Maybe they can help me look for Gypsy too."

"Wait a minute. You mean those two boys who went out on their horse and died in the snowstorm? Except the horse never left them. The Jones boys?" It was Meggie now. "Those two boys buried up in the Comstock cemetery in Gold Hill?"

"They're my family. And I feel like maybe Jennica is, too. Or at least she's the best friend I ever had. I have to go back. I have to help her. I can't leave Jennica."

"The Jones boys?" Paige said, shaking her head in confusion. "Their horse still circles their grave. The Haunted Horse won't leave the Virginia range. He won't leave the boys."

"*The Haunted Horse of Gold Hill*," Meggie said the words slowly, carefully. "Oh my gosh. Nobody is going to believe this."

"Wait a minute, Brooks. The police or the sheriff might arrest us for letting you go like this." Paige inched closer, digging into her jeans for her cell phone. "You can't go. If you do, I'll call 911."

"You can't stop me, Paige. Besides, they don't have to know where I've gone. You can just tell them I left. And just tell the family where I'm staying in Virginia City that I had to move on. Which is true."

Meggie's chin fell and she reached toward Paige. "Let him go, Paige."

Brooks backed up. "But I'll miss you guys," he said to them both. "And I'll let you know when we find Gypsy. I promise."

"How can you do that when we have to leave in a few days?" Paige grabbed his arm. "There won't be enough time to find Gypsy and get back to us."

"Time changes as soon as I crawl through the trunk. Time isn't going to matter, Paige." He turned and hurried toward N° 9, un-latching the visitor chain and jumping in.

"Besides, we need you Brooks," she called to him with unsteady words. "The Ghostowners won't be the same without you!"

He paused and turned, that familiar slow smile creeping up one side of his face. "Remember, Paige. I'm too old to be an authentic Ghostowner."

Paige drew a quick breath and frowned. "I changed my mind."

"Let him go," Meggie said again, backing away.

## Chapter Thirteen

"Sorry Brooks left without even saying goodbye," Russ said on their last day as volunteers at the museum. "I suppose he's back in Virginia City with the family he's been staying with?"

"He might be," Paige said with wide, glassy eyes. It was possible. She backed away slowly, not wanting any more questions.

Meggie leaned against the brass rail as her best friend walked up. "It's our last day and they haven't returned," she said to Paige. "This is really sad."

Paige nodded. "I know. Way too sad to think we might never know—never see them again."

"Brooks promised," she replied, fingering her ponytail absently. Suddenly something caught her eye. She jerked around and gasped, staring at car N° 9.

"Meggie!" Paige cried out, running toward the passenger car on display. "It's them!"

Meggie Bryson almost fell over her best friend. "Jennica! Brooks!" she cried out, staring at the golden-haired girl in her old fashioned coat dancing with Brooks and laughing.

"He's such a klutz, Meggie!" Paige cried, laughing through her tears. "He's tripping all over her feet!"

"Oh, my gosh—look, Paige. She's holding Gypsy. They found Gypsy!"

But Paige hadn't noticed. "Jennica! Brooks!" she cried, racing toward car N° 9.

Jennica smiled and waved and then threw them a kiss. And suddenly they were gone.

Meggie fell over her feet and crashed into Paige.

"They're gone. Just like that. Gone," Paige choked out the words.

"Yes," Meggie said. "But they found Gypsy. At least they found Gypsy."

"I didn't see Gypsy," she said to Meggie, her eyes wide and glistening.

"Jennica was holding him Paige."

"I don't believe it," Paige said, getting up from the floor. "You just imagined it." She brushed some dust off her jeans angrily. "It's something you just want to believe. Something we both want to believe."

Meggie climbed into N° 9, her pulse pounding. "No. No, I saw Gypsy. That little dog had that bone in his mouth. Gypsy was smiling almost. I swear it, Paige."

"If only it was true," Paige said, leaning against the railroad car, brushing away unwanted tears.

Suddenly Meggie exploded into a yell that echoed from one end of the railroad museum to the other. "Look!" she screamed. "LOOK!"

Paige leaped into the railroad car and saw the little rawhide bone lying on the wooden floor. She stood beside Meggie, wide-eyed. Stunned.

Paige and Meggie stared dumbfounded at the words carved on the little bone almost a hundred and fifty years before.

*BELIEVE*

"Closing up!" Mr. Walker called out, his cowboy boots clicking on the polished floor as he walked toward the Ghostowners in N° 9.

They stood unmoving, overwhelmed.

"Hey," he went on, "what's going on? You two act like you've seen a ghos…" Suddenly, he paused. "Wait a minute, did you finally see her? The Ghost Girl?"

"Yes," Meggie said through dry lips, fidgeting with her ponytail.

"Except she's not a ghost," Paige said to him.

Meggie wiped a stray tear from her wide blue eyes and nodded. "She's an angel."

Paige bit her lip and bent down to pick up Gypsy's bone, smiling so wide inside she thought she might burst. *Thank you, Brooks and Jennica. Thank you, Gypsy.*

*You're welcome.*

# EPILOGUE

The Nevada State Orphan's Asylum was opened in Virginia City in May 1867 by Sister Frederica McGrath and two other nuns of the Sisters of Charity. Eventually taken over by the state of Nevada and relocated to Carson City, the Nevada State Children's Home served as Nevada's home for dependent and neglected children until 1963.

### Robert "Pony Bob" Haslam

 Born in 1840 in London England, Robert "Pony Bob" Haslam is known for having made the longest and most courageous ride on the Pony Express, carrying mail and covering 380 treacherous miles across Nevada in two days.

In 1860 the Pony Express began, hiring young men who were tough, brave and hard-working; men who pledged not to drink alcohol, use profanity, or get into fights, but above all, men who were first-rate horsemen. Wages, $50 a month. Robert Haslam was one such man. He came to the United States as a teen and before long found work building the express stations and was later assigned the 75-mile ride between Friday's Station (the State Line) to Buckland Station near Fort Churchill. Once the telegraph lines linked East and West in 1861, the need for the Pony Express ended and eventually Robert Haslam went to work for the Wells Fargo Company. Later he served as Deputy U.S. Marshal in Salt Lake City and eventually moved to Chicago where he lived until his death in 1912 at the age of 72.

### Hank Monk

 Henry "Hank" Monk was born in New York in 1826, moving to California in 1852 to begin driving stage between Sacramento and Auburn for the California Stage Company. He always had a fancy for horses and in 1857 went to Nevada and drove stage between Placerville and Genoa, (then the metrop-

olis of the state) driving Nevada Stages for more than twenty years.

Monk is described as incomparable, the most daring, the most reckless of drivers; and the luckiest. In his prime Monk would turn a six-horse coach in the street with the team at full speed, and with every rein apparently loose. But the coach would always end up in exactly the spot that the most skillful driver would have tried to bring it. Hank Monk had a peculiar drawl and was reserved of speech except when battling a high-strung team or a stubborn, dignified passenger over the Sierras. The daring ride over the mountains with the famous Horace Greeley proved that the man outside the vehicle was perhaps as big as the one inside.

Henry "Hank" Monk died of pneumonia in Carson City in 1883 at the age of 57.

### John "Snowshoe" Thompson

"Snowshoe" Thompson, known as the "Viking of the Sierra" became a legend in Nevada and California history. He was born in 1827 on a mountainside farm in Norway, settling finally in his ranch home in Diamond Valley, California with his wife Agnes and son Arthur. For over twenty years, "Snowshoe" braved 20 to 50-foot snow depths, snow drifts and blizzards between Placerville California and Genoa Nevada, carrying a 50 to 100-pound mailbag, medicines, and supplies for neighbors and friends. Courageous and strong, he rode his homemade "long" skis over the high Sierra mountain ridges using a single pole for balance, carrying crackers and dried beef for food and drinking melted snow from his hand. The mail and supplies were Genoa's only contact with the outside world during the long winter months. In his lifetime he received little recognition or material reward for his courage and loyalty.

Snowshoe Thompson died of pneumonia from an appendicitis attack in 1876 and is buried beside his wife and son in the Genoa cemetery. Carved, crossed skis mark the headstone of this true hero of the Old West.

·

Car N° 9 was built in February 1873 by the Kimball Manufacturing Company of San Francisco at a cost of $1,900. In addition to bench seating down the length of the car, there was a separate area for baggage and express items. After the Comstock boom years, the V & T remodeled N° 9 as a bunk car for carpenter crews who maintained and repaired railroad buildings and bridges. In 1913, the car was rebuilt a second time as a traditional caboose with a center cupola. This car was sold to Paramount Pictures in 1938 and was featured in the Cecil B. DeMille movie *Union Pacific* and other motion pictures. The cupola was removed during its movie career. The Nevada State Railroad Museum restored car N° 9 to its original configuration, including the brass spittoons in the floor. The baggage section contains several old trunks and suitcases.

*The Haunted Horse of Gold Hill* (The Brooks Jones story)
www.Amazon.com    www.CalamityJan.com